The Lion and the Library

Mary Catelli

Published by Wizard's Wood Press, 2015.

This is a work of fiction. Similarities to real people, places, or events are entirely coincidental.

THE LION AND THE LIBRARY

First edition. June 21, 2015.

Copyright © 2015 Mary Catelli.

The Lion and the Library

The library, filled with lore and legends and lawsuits, had stout stone walls, thick enough to shield the silence within from any tumult. One could wade through accounts of campaigns against monsters, and chronicles of enchanted gems, without learning of any troubles outside.

Lena, pouring over papers by the light of her sundrop, searching through musty parchments for lions and kings, only slowly realized how long she had done it without Erion's arriving. When it finally dawned on her, she looked about.

From the high windows, the sparse light pierced out, as it did morn or eve or noontide, high overhead; the scholars used sundrops for good reason. Drably clad scholars spoke in low voices, glided among the stacks with sundrops glowing in their hands, or bent over the desks, but they did not include Erion. She knew that, in her bones, before she noted that no one wore a scarf of bright blue, with white stars woven in.

No one else, that was. She fingered her scarf. Erion would have sought her out.

Feeling a cold dread, Lena forced her breath in and out. She could not forfeit the freedom of the library, whatever the news would be. She had proved it useful many times. And—it hurt to think it but—it would be all the more if she became the only one with the freedom, if Erion could not come.

She moved stiffly, gathering up the documents, and swallowed. Erion himself would not approve of her losing it.

Lena blinked against the sunlight. As at dawn so now as well—a bright and cloudless day. The street held fewer people than she had ever seen it, and none were Celestians; she could not see another scarf such as hers for the length of it.

A crowd, full of wailing, surged down the street like waters suddenly freed from a dam. Every one of them wore the scarf. Lena swallowed. The few Solarians on the street eyed the Celestians and for once stepped aside, to avoid this distraught flood. Lena tried to pick out someone, anyone, that she knew, her gaze flitting over them. She did not think there was a woman among them who had her headdress on quite straight.

One woman, despite her reddened eyes, looked, despairingly, at the library. Her mother Mirjam, Lena realized with surprise, and then her mother scrambled up the stairs to her, with no heed for whether anyone went up or down the stairs about her. Her little sister Anila wailed and ran after. Half a dozen other women joined in. Eyes of blue, or violet, looked at her in distress. Lena felt a cold weight lodge in her stomach.

But her mother had her hands. "O my darling, my dove—you must be brave—you must listen—" Tears splattered down her cheek. "Better to hear at once and be done!"

Anila scrambled up beside her, and clung to Lena's arm.

"That evil one, the king's councilor Kudret—he predicted evil days for the king, for King Halis."

Lena felt almost numb. The king. He would do evil of sheer spite if evil befell him. But whatever evil had fallen, they could only suffer and endure; they could do nothing.

Her mother's words inched out. "He went to pick a king out."

Lena felt like ice. She managed to move her mouth. "But not from among the criminals?"

Of course not, came a cool thought. Even in this city, it would take more than a morning to catch Erion and convict him of some crime. Had King Halis chosen such a king, Erion would have joined her, and this crowd would not have formed. . . .

She shuddered. Always before, the kings had gone to avert ill luck by choosing a condemned man to act as king, and take the ill luck, and be executed. She had read the scrolls, heard the tales, exclaimed with the rest beside the hearth—but now it was not some fireside tale. Not when she already knew who had been chosen to suffer at the guards' hands all the days unlucky for the king, and then to be executed at the end.

Her mother babbled on, on how the king had had Kudret summon all the Celestian men, and the women had come to learn the evil news, and Kudret had chosen one. And then could not speak, as if she actually had to reveal the news.

"It's Erion." With great violet eyes, Anila looked solemnly up at her.

Her legs folded under her. She sat on the steps, staring outward, her breath shallow and fast. She had known, she had known, but to hear it was a nightmare. The women fussed about her, and scholars coming out grumbled about the crowd, and both felt like something poking at an unhealed wound. She shuddered.

"Madness," muttered her Aunt Bela, a couple of steps below. "We'll never—I barely managed to wangle the betrothal to him! She'll die unwed for sure."

The slap across her face rang out. Lena, breathing hard, realized that she had stood and glared back at her aunt's bewildered gaze.

"Come." Old Klarita's voice rose from the street, and though she bore a staff, she stood over it like an ancient oak. "We go to King Halis, to reproach him with having set that one, Kudret, to choose his substitute."

Always before the king had chosen a condemned criminal, not from among the Celestians. Nevertheless, as she adjusted her headdress, ensured that her hair was covered by the scarf, Lena felt as barren and bleak as the cold sands of a northern desert that had never known snow. She would go to this court because never again might she have the chance to see Erion.

That thought, sword-like, sliced through her numbness. With half a hundred memories of Erion, from his handing her a nosegay of pale blue spring flowers, to reading together over an ancient scroll of righteous kings, to his standing before her father, solemn, to ask for her hand in marriage.

Tears welled up in her eyes. The shifting crowd bore her along.

Celestians gathered like birds descending after winter, though their whispers were softer than the birds' twittering. Here, even more pitying glances fell on her. She felt too fraught with bitter pain to care. Erion, Erion—she would not care to marry if he died—

If? She let her mother and sister bundle her forward—the crowd parted for them—and only wallowed in her folly. If! As if King Halis would regard it as anything but a fate a Celestian had earned!

They stopped. She realized that they had brought her to below the dais, where she could see all, and be seen. Just where, perhaps, his parents might have stood if Erion had not been an orphan— Her mother took one of her hands. Anila took the other. And King Halis appeared on the balcony, beneath the roof that shadowed his royal scarlet until it looked not like fresh blood, but dark blood from a mortal wound.

A murmur came through the crowd. Lena saw the guards in dark armor and got a glimpse, but only a glimpse, of the gold and royal scarlet before she docilely bowed her head with the rest.

When she raised it again, the crowd had parted, far more readily than it had for her. The first guards still lashed out with their staffs, inflicting bruises and blood on the pretense of clearing the way. In the center of the clump, Erion walked, in gold and scarlet robes, and in chains. His face was grave and set, and he did not glance to either side. His lip showed blood, and the side of his face, a bruise. He did not falter, but a guard still shoved him onward. She could not see all the gemstones they bore on wristbands or sword hilts, but she saw enough tiger's eyes. Erion could not flee past their sight.

Anila squeaked. Lena looked down. Her knuckles had grown white with her grip. She loosened her fingers—it felt like freeing manacles that had held for centuries—and forced her breath in and out. They could not misuse him too badly, or he would not live to suffer execution, only at the end of the unlucky days.

In the shadows of the Queen's Niche, something moved. Lena blinked. That foreign princess Pulcherie sprawled there, a pale shadow, and her attendants hovered about her like birds about a new hatchling, and Lena hated her.

A light pattering of feet drew her eyes aside again. An old man, lean like a cricket, his hair paler than sunlit clouds, wore not the blue scarfs that others did, but a robe with stars and the moon woven in. He ran down the cleared path. Though the guards had already hauled Erion before the balcony, the crowd murmured and stayed back for him.

"Petrit," said Lena.

"The hermit?" said Anila, sharply. Their mother hushed her, but Lena kept her eyes on Petrit. It would indeed take a miracle to aid them. Petrit did not glance aside and stopped only at the dais. The king, his eyes narrowed, studied him.

"A terrible fate awaits you, o king!" Petrit's voice rang from the building, and her stomach roiled. Encourage King Halis to think of his own danger? Erion looked away, as if regally dismissing the hermit from his thoughts, and stood with his face set like flint.

"A dreadful fate will befall you on those days—you will become a murderer!"

Petrit swept his hand toward the sky. "It is the fate of men under the sun to suffer illness and accident, but no man is forced to shed innocent blood. That is the fate you may yet avoid."

King Halis's lip curled. "This is no time for a mountebank to try to amuse me." His hand moved downward through the air like a headsman's axe. The guards headed toward Petrit.

"To add to your sins to silence them—is to pile folly on folly," said Petrit, and to Lena's relief, drew back so quickly that the guards stayed to guard the king.

The king surveyed the crowd.

Zenil stepped forward and bowed. He had prospered as a merchant, but his clothing showed only a touch of his wealth in the fineness of the cloth. His face showed even less fear.

"Your Majesty," he said, his voice deep and grave, "you astound me. Alas, the prisons burst with those deserving of death, and yet you must choose a man guilty of no crime?"

"How," said King Halis, sounding almost as grave, "could I inflict such a king on my people?"

Zenil's face spasmed, but a moment later, unable to say that the pretended king would have no power, he said, "For your sake, Your Majesty, we could endure it."

King Halis hesitated.

"Do not do it," said Kudret, smoothly, at the king's elbow. "Do not even consider it. How, Your Majesty, is suffering a just execution *misfortune*? The one who must take your place must suffer those days' misfortune." He shook his head. "There are kings who foolishly chose murderers to take their place, and the ill luck was not averted."

Because it is a foolish superstition, thought Lena. Both the foretelling and the foolish attempt to avert it.

Kudret's voice rolled smoothly on. "A king must consider how his fate affects his kingdom."

King Halis nodded.

"Besides—a Celestian! He insults the Unconquerable Sun!" Kudret swept a hand toward Erion. "Look at him. Even his own eyes warn him that he should have turned aside from his ways!"

His tone grew warmer, and his words more swift. "Why, it would be better for him to suffer death to save Your Majesty, than if the Sun withheld the mercy he has extended so long, and completed what he began, by turning the knave into a bird, or a fish, or a cat, as he has already begun by giving him their eyes." Kudret drew a deep breath. "But then, who can understate their folly, who see daily the radiance of the Unconquerable Sun, and yet deny it for some—thing that can not be seen?"

"How true," said King Halis, coldly.

"But, Your Majesty," said old Vidrum, a silver-haired scribe limping forward, "how can you speak so heartlessly before his very betrothed?"

Every gaze followed his gesture toward her, and she hoped she looked lovely and anguished—before she doubted. Would he have been less monstrous to have chosen among the widowed or the unbetrothed? He would just choose another, if he heeded Vidrum's appeal.

King Halis looked troubled. Her heart leapt, for all her doubts.

A sigh came out of the Queen's Niche, heard only in the silence. "O my heart, o the soul of my life." Even for this, Queen Pulcherie's voice sounded languid. "O, do not risk yourself, do not imperil yourself, do not endanger yourself—I can not bear it, think of my love and do not harm my heart—"

King Halis twitched, like a horse throwing off a fly.

"Enough of these appeals. This wretch has been called to an honor far beyond his desert. He shall do his duty. Whoever seeks to stay me shall not see him perish, for he shall die first!"

He looked at Erion, and got Erion's steady gaze back. He flinched, but—he would not change his will.

Abed, Lena studied the ceiling's whitewash. Her arms sprawled on the mattress, her face felt slack, and nothing stirred any desire to move in her. Grayish sunlight seeped into the room. She closed her eyes. No one would rouse her if she did not stir.

No one would venture to the library to find anything that might aid Erion, as she and Erion had found that water stone, if she did not stir.

And if no sober history would tell of such aid, neither had any such history told of the water stone.

There was still the lion and its heart. For a moment, her mouth twisted. Perhaps the king had lied, and Erion had been chosen for his knowledge of it. She doubted it. The king's minsters and the king himself did not think highly of the scholars, to listen to them, and the scholars did not think of highly of Erion, to learn what he searched for. She, and she alone, knew.

Lena sighed. Then she swung her legs off the bed and pushed herself up to stand, blinking like an owlet, with her shift falling to her ankles. She would hate the library. There was not a shelf there that would not remind her of Erion.

Dress first, she thought, and found every step of it required thought to move her hands through it. Over her shift, her smock. Her overdress, and to lace that up—it took concentration to tighten up the ribbons, and five times as long as she needed with her wits about her. Her coat. Her mantle. Sit on the bed to don stocking and shoe. Up again to brush out her hair and be glad they could afford no such frivolity as a mirror. She reached for her headdress.

As she adjusted the combs to hold it on, Anila started at the door.

"Oh, you're up."

Lena pushed the comb firmly in place. "It is the king who is Erion's misfortune. He will not hear that my grief slew me even before his own death."

Anila blinked.

Lena headed out, and down the narrow stair to the kitchen. Porridge. Though her betrothed lay under sentence of death, some of her gloom was hunger.

Her mother looked up from the porridge pot. "You look ready for the street."

"I am going to the library. To look—"

Aunt Bela hooted. "Library? What help is the library? No law will protect us, and were there twenty—a hundred—laws and more, the king would ignore them all."

She rambled on, and Lena passed her to take the bowl her mother gave her. If she had held her tongue, she might not have had to suffer until her escape to the street.

Bela threw her hands into the air. "It's utterly useless!"

Lena ate, did not lift her gaze from the bowl, and was glad she had not told all. Bela would jeer all the more if she had said she did not go to piece together futile law, but legend.

She, and Erion, had found the water stone that way. She stood and laid aside the bowl. For a moment, she stared down at her hands, still on it, and remembered the transparent stone, the lightest of greens, and how it had for a moment glinted among the dark rounded rocks of the dry spring, before water had come to cover all, and make all glint.

She pulled her hands away. Her family had paid the dowry of four daughters out of the money for that. But now she wanted something greater than that.

In the cloudy day, the street held as many people as ever, scurrying about, wearing the blue scarf by law, but though they went about their business, they seemed subdued. Even the haggling went on in low voices, and most of it seemed to be for food. Insults to each other's ancestors or diet did not resounded the length of the street at all, let alone every few minutes. No one stopped on a corner to talk. Even the women waiting to draw water did not chatter among themselves.

Lena scurried with the rest, down narrow streets, still overshadowed by the dingy buildings, neither gray nor brown, that lined the street. Bela had had this much right: Erion had not found a clear document, but one he had asked her to look at as well. To be sure, he had not thought the Lion's Heart a certainty to be more than a curious legend. But any magic that could defend the innocent—what other hope did she have? And the danger to her was not terrible. If she failed, she might escape all notice, and only Erion would suffer.

Anguish nearly doubled her over. She fought to steady her breath. How Bela would scold her—such unseemly devotion for her to feel before the marriage ceremony. Even her mother would gravely disapprove. She forced her breath out. She should have, she told herself, seek this legend out whomever Kudret had chosen.

Though Erion's aid would have made it easier, had the choice fallen on any other.

She fled down the street over the cobblestones as if she could outrun the pain.

Three corners later, she reached a street more busy, with fewer of the blue scarfs. She slowed before she collided and caused offense. Her breath came as harshly as if wolves had chased her over a mountainside. Some passersby glanced at her, perhaps in recognition, perhaps just noting the scarf and the Celestian, whose disfavor at law they had recently been reminded of. She forced her breath to ease. Stealth and silence would be needed allies if she were to succeed at all.

A church along the way gleamed with gold and candlelight, as brilliant as the sun on a clear day. Songs resounded, sonorously. Lena crept to the other side alongside, unable to close her ears to the prayers of petition for the king's wellbeing and the triumph of averting evil from him.

Lena did not even look over.

She had to put her sundrop down on the shelf to keep the light from trembling over the scrolls like sunlight through wind-shaken leaves. She smoothed out the parchment with double care. Erion had not been foolish to ask her to look at it again. If he had not spoken of it, she would have wondered whether the scrolls had really talked of the lions of legend in their poetic lines about perfection and rubies.

And justice. Above all else, the legends spoke of justice. But first she had to deal with perfection and ruby, and at that, she could only pray that a teeming royal city did not hold two perfect rubies of that size.

In spite of herself, her mouth twitched. Or perhaps that the Master of Heavens would guide her steps to the right one, no matter how many the city held.

Her gaze drifted over the room, the shadows, the motes of light in a sunbeam, the shelves and shelves and shelves of books. Her breath came out as she remembered standing here, and Erion speaking to her. Grave, composed, as if he had feared that anything less dignified would inspire her to take him for a fool, telling her they could find the way, into the treasury, by routes the Solarians would fear to tread. In these books.

She did not need to read them all. She had even read, before, many ones that she wanted now. Then she had laid them aside because venturing to the tunnels had been rash and useless.

It was not yet useful. Her teeth worried her lower lip. She had time. Indeed, she had to take her time, to await the hour of Erion's coronation, before she struck.

Still, she rolled up the scroll, to go and claim another. Using the days and hours to take care would be wiser, especially as she had to commit her route to memory. She walked among the soft-voiced scholars and among the shelves. This route she had already mastered.

A soft cough sounded. At the end of those shelves, Rodvan stood. Another man stood by him—dark as Rodvan was, with features alike as well, and young, perhaps younger than she was. She looked back, her eyes narrowed, and her hand lingered on the scroll.

He's just, said a sly thought. *He knows your great grief. He won't hold it against you.*

She sighed, and her shoulders slumped. She almost wished, as she came forward, that she could ask him for aid, but for all his graciousness to her and to Erion, Rodvan remained a Solarian.

And probably could do nothing for either of them, at that.

"I rejoice to see you in good health," said Rodvan, his voice formal, his deer-dark eyes solemn. "My son has returned from abroad in good health, and bearing books that perhaps will interest you."

Lena bowed her head and murmured politeness on his return.

"They talk of allowing only Solarians to view them."

For a moment, Lena could not breathe. Such blind pettiness, to corner her to tell her that—she would never have dreamed—

"My daughter—" His voice was very heavy. "—you should consider your folly. Surely even you have suffered to see the imprudence—"

"I—" Her voice was as harsh as a crow's, but it silenced him. She swallowed. "I can not foreswear the Master of Heaven and Earth, to whom I owe my being, and who has set my feet on this path."

Rodvan said, "The Sun is the source of all being—it can plainly be seen—even the stars and the moon are but its shadows—how could a being that can not even be seen have more power than the Glorious Sun?"

Her face set.

A moment after, with a nod of his head, he stepped aside. His son bowed and went with him. Tunnels, Lena reminded herself, with a bitter taste in her mouth, and the sour thought that Rodvan spoke out of nothing but kindness.

She still had to go in the same direction that Rodvan had gone. She walked with all the dignity she could muster, and the son, in a voice almost low enough that she could not hear, told his father that he should wait until her great grief had receded.

Feeling cold, hollow, and alone, she turned down one row, not even able to feel glad that she followed them no longer. Perhaps her aunt Bela would be pleased, though Rodvan would not, of course, venture to propose a betrothal so soon, or even once Erion was decently dead but not long in his grave.

And he would never, of course, even think of his son's becoming a Celestian to wed her, however otherwise fit she was as a bride.

She slept restlessly that night; every time she drifted into slumber, dreams of rubies—rubies larger than her joined fists, dark as garnets or heart's blood, looming in darkness—woke her again, leaving her panting and horrified past reason. Once, she leaned back against her pillow and wondered if the dreams bore warnings. She stared out into the unanswering darkness.

Across the room, Anila shifted and sighed. At least, her sister slept like a log, and she would not have to explain why she slept so restlessly. . . .

Though she would not have. Anila would think them dreams of Erion, and ask no questions.

Lena could feel the bitterness in her smile. And then memory slid to Erion with an ancient scroll in hand, pointing her to how a perfect ruby would not only glow of its own, like a coal, but how it could work magic.

Anila, perched on the hearth with her mending, looked brightly up at Lena. "It can't be that hard, Lena. You and Erion both looked on your own in less than a year." She waved a hand in the air. "You had to ask questions after, but don't all of the scholars have to ask *sometimes*?"

Lena forced her breath in and out. Behind her, their mother moved about with the clean breakfast dishes. She said nothing, though she must have heard Anila's talk, and her question. Likely, she thought that training Anila would distract Lena nicely, even at the risk of having a second bookish daughter.

Lena swallowed. Her mother would be no help, but she still had to refuse. Hard enough that Rodvan might spy what she did. Anila would be all over it in moments if she were in the library.

"It's work," she said. "Hard work. It takes much searching to find anything useful."

"Like the waterstone. That must have been wonderful to watch, but I didn't get to see it."

Lena remembered. The stone, clear as air, pale green, flashing in Erion's hand as he threw it down among the dry stones—the water that rose as smoothly as a mist—the next morning, when she had roused from her sleep in the shepherds' hut to see the streamside covered with flowers like blue stars, and the oldest shepherds declaring that they had indeed seen such blossoms, when they were children—and she could only hope that she had not exhausted her ability to find marvels. She still had the crown of flowers that Erion had woven for her, but it was so dried that the colors were little more than memories.

Anila tugged her sleeve, to grab her attention. "And if I worked anywhere else," she said triumphantly, "I'd work just as hard, and never even have a chance to see such a thing."

Lena's mouth tightened. "I haven't—I can't train you quickly enough."

"There is that," said their mother, quietly, from the doorway. Lena glanced over, and flinched. Before her stood Solok and

Klarita, and they had not only arrived uncommonly early to visit and gossip, but both women eyed her as avidly as a beggar would a feast.

"But," her mother continued, "you would have to start some time. It is best to keep busy in evil times." Her mouth curved, though nothing else in her face smiled.

"Oh yes oh yes," murmured Solok and Klarita together, their heads bobbing up and down like leaves buffeted by a wind as they edged into the room. Lena, wary, circled around them.

"It's so dreadful," said Solok. "Parading him about like the king had actually chosen his heir. So ghastly."

"And the bruises!" said Klarita. "You'd think the guards were trying to beat him to death before the day." She shuddered. "*So* dreadful."

"I have to go now," said Lena. "The sooner I finish the tasks I have to do alone, the sooner I can train Anila." Her hand reached for the doorframe, and she forced it down and into a fist before she could try to steady herself before those two ghouls. Her mother looked severe, and she fled.

Behind her, their voices rose again, shrilly discussing how much harder it would be for Lena alone, perhaps she should not venture to such hard duties. . . .

Beneath the cloudy sky, in the chilly air, she hurried. She had no need to go to the library. To read every scroll and codex a seventh time would not make them yield up new secrets, and hunting about for more would reap little. She had preparations to make, but putting them off until the last minute would mean she had less time to hide them. Perhaps she could have taught Anila in the meantime.

A blast of wind gusted down the street, pulling at her skirt.

She had given her excuse already, and it would be unwise to undermine it. And she might find more knowledge, and she doubted she could keep herself from searching. And the farther

Anila was from her work, the better—if only to keep her from
betraying her, or being stained by her deeds.

Thunder grumbled, far off in the distance, and she let out her
breath. She should look for other knowledge. Another thing like
the waterstone would aid even if her plan utterly failed, and Erion
died.

A raindrop splattered against the cobblestones, leaving a trace
larger than many coins. Lena hurried up the stairs toward the
door, not so quickly as to avoid the rainfall that speckled the street
like a leopard's skin, but she stepped within before it did more than
splatter. She hurried deeper inside, and the rain hurled itself
against the roof, so heavily that single drops could not be made out
in the clatter.

She had good reason not to return any time soon.

She glanced up. Despite decades of grime, on the ceiling, the
lapis lazuli blue with its gilt sun, the black with silver moon and
stars, glinted to remind her that the library had once been a
Celestian church. She let her breath out. The Master of Heavens
could still guide her steps here.

Those scholars who moved about the vast room did so as
gravely as ever, but far fewer of them than usual, and so the light
was more dim, with so few sundrops. Lena moved across the floor,
as silently as she could, as always.

Down one bookcase, Rodvan inspected a scroll. Then his gaze
caught hers, and he jumped and shoved it away. Lena stood still a
moment. Without his movement, she would never have noted
where he stood, at what he looked, but that scroll had been among
those she had looked at.

And gawking like this had told him that she had guessed that.
She turned her face away and walked on, as the rain resounded,
overhead. She could hope that he would not guess before she
could strike, or even that his fondness for a bright young scholar
would dissuade him from acting against her.

She found the shelf she sought, but she had to draw a breath to steady herself before she took up a codex. Despite everything, she would be glad when Erion's mockery of a coronation was over. She could do so little before then.

Though not nothing.

In the gloomy vault, her heart pattered. She hurried over the floor's flagstones.

When desecrating the church, the Solarians had kept no records of it. If she had not visited the books that an old Celestian scholar had kept privately, she would never have known what was stored down here, and how it was guarded.

Which meant good hope of finding it still there.

The jug of water sweated in her hands, and left a trail of dark splatters behind her. Her fingers tightened on its neck, though they had started to numb. She had drawn it straight from a spring for its bone-chilling cold, and now—her gaze darted about. She could see if it could not—

A soft hiss resounded. Lena glanced about again. The scales were brown and barely caught the light, but the snake glided over the stone. Its blind head turned to and fro as it sought out the heat that had roused it.

Lena put one hand to the jug bottom to hold it more firmly. The snake slithered closer. She tilted the jug and flung the water, spraying both snake and stone. The guardian recoiled from the chill, and Lena ran past it, deeper into the vaults, clutching the jug to her as if it were a child.

With the snake behind her, she slowed. Even after she caught her breath, her heart hammered, but she did not stop. The light shone no more brightly than starlight would, but she could picked her way. Her mouth twitched. She held out the jug again, away from her, though the water in it sloshed. Her clothes were already wet. She could only hope that it would dry after she found her way down, and back.

"Commend your cares and whatever troubles your heart," she whispered, "to the trusty hands of Him Who set the stars. He who set the heavens in order and appointed their hours will also find paths where your feet can walk."

After a moment, she smiled. Of course the water had worked. The snake was the guardian of a treasury, where they wished to go in and out if they needed the treasures; they needed some way to stop its poison; it could not be too difficult.

The doorway loomed before her. It was not much larger than she was, but even against this gloom, it seemed dark. Carefully, Lena set down the jug—it took a moment to steady it on the rough floor —and, looking away, drew out the sundrop.

It still blinded as light flooded the vault and cast her enormous shadow against the stones.

Lena blinked. Moments later, she held the stone to one side and picked her way into the secret chamber. Even through her watering eyes, she made out glints here and there—treasures that a conqueror could have had, if only he had been less bloodthirsty, or had not treated scholars as less than dead leaves blown by the wind.

She looked past them. Gold and jewels would not buy Erion's life. She dashed her hand over her eyes, and a silvery gleam caught her gaze, long enough for her to make out the rope. Her breath stole out. Gold and jewels could last long, down in this snake-guarded labyrinth, but only enchantment could preserve a rope of spider silk. To still be here showed that it was what the parchments had said.

Lena slipped closer, realizing she felt more fearful than delighted, but nonetheless, she reached out. Her fingers closed on the rope. Though smoother than any rope she had ever touched before—and most thread—it felt solid, and lifting it from the shelf meant only that flopped down from her hand, not that it crumbled into dust.

"You read too many legends," she charged herself.

The echoes died about her. A hiss sounded from the doorway.

For a moment, she felt as if she had plunged head first into the spring herself. She whipped about. The snake lifted its blind head to lick the air and hiss again. Even as her mouth went dry, it slithered past the jug.

Too far, too far, she thought, stumbling backward. The vault did not hold enough room for her to be sure of running about it—her waist struck one shelf—even were the snake not heading toward her like a slow but well-aimed arrow.

The rope fell from her fingers, and her hand fumbled back and closed about something like a handle. Blindly, she threw it.

The knife pierced its head. For a moment, it strained against it, and its coils thrashed about as the blood bubbled. Not red blood. Blacker than starless midnight. Lena fought down her panic, but the snake had fallen still before she had mastered it. Still breathing light and fast, she crouched to take up the rope and sling it over her shoulder before she inched toward the door.

The knife handle, she thought, looked like bone. She swallowed a laugh for fear of what would follow, and a stray thought idly said, "He will find paths where your feet can walk."

She stood a minute longer. This was the treasury. What it contained was well worth the protections of the vault. No one would be fool enough to place a commonplace knife here.

Picking her way about the dead coils and the black pool of blood, telling herself that she did so for fear of betraying bloodstains, she found a stretch of stone close enough to reach.

The knife came free too easily, considering the skull it must have struck. Though it bore blood on the blade, it did not drip.

She scampered for the doorway. There, not knowing whether there were more snakes, she slid away the sundrop. The gloom returned.

Moments later, her eyes seeing as much as they could, she bent to take up the jug and lugged it along as she crept through the labyrinth again.

When the light had increased again, even past what the stone could shed, Lena braced herself and looked at the knife again. The blood, still damp, looked not black but deep purple.

She winced and put down the jug to wash the blade with the last of the water. The rope she would hide here until the hour to strike. The knife—the knife she would carry with her. It was small enough to hide.

A strange hum, like a vast beehive, filled the city on the eve of the coronation. Even among the Solarians, it did not sound only of excitement. Still, she had to walk among them, on her way.

Her stomach felt like a mob of butterflies. Wherever she went, silence and gazes followed her, followed by sibilant whispers. She tried to walk calmly, as if she were nothing more than she had been, but while the words did not carry, the fascination in them did. As if Erion's first decree would be to summon her and make her his queen, and partaker of his fate. As if the coronation would grant Erion the power to make decrees.

She looked up at the library.

"You fool! Courting your doom!"

A hermit pressed through the crowd—dirtier and more ragged than Petrit—aimed utterly at her. Every passerby shifted from his path; some looked at him with fear; he ignored every one of them.

"You, venturing there still? After what befall Erion? It was no more than the justice." He threw his hands in the air. "To walk on the floors dedicated to the Most High, to the Master of Heavens, as if it were meant to house mere parchments!"

Lena flinched back. I need—I aid Celestians—but she kept her tongue. To encourage him would be worse folly. She looked about for a clear way. She saw no signs of guards, and flinched away from that thought. Even this madman did not deserve what the guards would do if they caught him.

"Do not tell me that we profit from your *scholarship*!"

Her heart seemed to stop, and then to hammer.

"Let the Solarians store up the wrath of the Master of Heavens for paltry coins! To go freely is to accept the desecration!"

She ran. Master of Heavens guide her, she ran with no heed to her footing, down streets—startling a flight of doves and drawing stares—around corners and over-laden donkeys, up stairs—at the height, the square held a fountain, plashing away, and Lena forced herself to stop. Her breath came harshly. A low wall blocked off the fall, and she leaned on it to steady herself. Vendors and passersby slowly stopped staring at her. Tales would probably spread about how Erion's bride had gone mad and run wild.

But not that she had gone into the library that had been a church. How could going there tell anyone anything when no one remembered it had been a church?

Three doves came slowly circling down. The first one, a shade of grayish brown that matched the stones, settled on the flagstones. Lena sighed. The other two followed. The brown of their breast was almost rosy.

If the Master of Heavens entrusted something small to you, such as entrance to the library, it was wise to use it wisely, lest he never entrust anything greater. She stood, straightened her head dress, and started down the stairs.

"Isn't her age enough?" Bela's sharp voice came through the kitchen door. Lena, uncommonly weary, hesitated in the shadowed street, though the moon already showed pale against the darkening sky, and the kitchen fire illuminated only a scrap of the flagstones. "Her oddities? The way she has always dressed like a widow just past mourning?"

Lena's mouth twitched. No one would hire a scholar not soberly dressed.

"Does she have to run down the city streets like a madwoman?"

Mirjam's voice was measured and dry. "Her great grief has turned her wits. We can easily explain her failure to wed, thus." A soft clatter spoke of her scraping some ingredient into a dish. "She can live with a sister, and her nieces will no doubt find her a figure from a ballad and even think that the king executed Erion out of jealousy."

Lena's mouth twisted. If ever a man was worth going mad for, it was Erion. She walked forward and softly announced her return.

Anila looked up from the pot on the hearth.

"Soup's near ready," she caroled.

"We shall have to eat well," said Lena. "The ceremony will be long, we will need our strength."

Because we will stand every moment of it. With the sky lowering lead gray over them, like the pall over a coffin.

Whoever was nearest her had murmured and looked at her. Some had urged her closer, as if the sight of a commonplace Celestian woman, like any other, would touch the king's heart—or as if she craved the sight of Erion's coronation.

She fingered her scarf. Between the dark buildings, every inch of cobblestone held the crowd, Solarian and Celestian. More Celestians, she thought, though who could judge with everyone on the level? A few bold souls leaned out of the lowest windows, but on some walls, even they risked being higher than the king.

Great bellowing cries of Henya! drew her gaze like a lodestone to the balcony. A crier, extravagant in violet and gold, proclaimed the great misfortune of the loss of King Halis, to be lamented by all below the sun—King Halis the brave, the wise, the prudent, the just, the temperate, the merciful, the generous, the magnanimous—

The crowd stood even more still and silent than usual for such a proclamation. Lena could not have sworn that she heard anyone breathe. A hawk's shrill cry, from where it circled, too high to be seen clearly, still resounded over them as if over a mountain valley where not even a flock of sheep grazed.

"Hence, a new king shall reign! May King Erion's virtues be as great as his predecessors!"

That, thought Lena, would not be difficult.

"And his reign as long and glorious!"

Lena shivered and pulled her mantle closer. She got only a glimpse of Erion as they hauled him forward, and forced herself to straighten. His robes were scarlet, heavily embroidered with gold, making his face look all the paler above them. Unbruised, Lena thought, and felt relief that she knew was madness. They had known what his coronation robes could not cover, and she could not know what injuries the robes could.

Bela whispered. "They got new robes to give King Halis, when he's crowned again. *Those* are cloth-of-gold."

Lena flinched.

At least Erion moved easily, she told herself. Servants moved about to disrobe him, down to the long white shirt—even on this cloudy day, it looked as bright as a wisp of cloud before the sun. The pallor of his hands and face blended insensibly with it.

And with him clad in this light attire, a hierophant in heavy white robes solemnly began the injunctions to rule wisely and well, and the duties of the righteous king, on and on and on, as if the abdication had slackened Halis's authority in the slightest. Even with Halis ensconced in the evening house—an old name for a tomb, and fitting for the palace where he would wait out this.

Wind blew over them. Lena shivered and wondered whether Erion was cold.

The invocation went on, but servants lifted the robes, to clad him in majesty.

They presented him with a sword, to deliver justice.

They crowned him with gold and ruby, to indicate rule.

They led him before the balcony, and called on the crowd to hail him as king.

Lena shouted with the rest and only after wondered how this false coronation could stir such a shout. Doves, startled, leapt from their perches and whirled through the air in great flocks. When the shout dwindled, their frantic coos echoed in its wake.

Aunt Bela's lip curled as she watched the flock. "Supposed to be a good sign, that. Supposed to mean a reign of peace."

Her voice was pitched so low that Anila looked up her, baffled. Lena swallowed, turned from the sky, and stared at Erion, knowing she might never see him again. Very likely that all his reign would know no war.

The crowd moved hesitantly at first, like ice half-clogging a spring river, but then they dispersed into the streets and alleyways. Lena almost wished she had worn an overmantle; to be thought overly pious and modest, hiding her face in shadow, would nonetheless be better than the pitying glances.

The sight of blue beside her made her blink and turn. Petrit looked gravely at her. Lena opened her mouth and shut it again.

"Do not despair, my daughter," he said. "Those who die do not depart from us forever. They go before us on a journey, which we must one day follow, as all men must."

Lena looked at him for a long minute, having no notion what she could say. Then, mutely, she bowed her head. He raised his hand to bless her.

Surely, she needed every blessing she could get.

"Better to have gone around," muttered Bela at the next stairs, where the swarm of people clumped again, waiting to descend.

Anila's nose wrinkled. "Like a donkey?"

"A donkey would be smarter than us, to forgo these stairs," said Mirjam. "It would be swifter, even if it would take us farther." She did not, however, shift from where she stood in the crowd.

Lena, abruptly feeling as if she could not breathe, broke free, out of the herd, to the empty flagstones past the crowd. Down the street ahead of her, people already vanished into their homes or their shops, free from the coronation and about their lives, leaving her all but alone on the stones. She drew in a deep breath.

"There she is!"

The voice boomed from high up; two stairs—both filled with people—stood between her and the soldiers staring down. Still, one pointed at her. They started to shove through the crowds, tossing people aside and ignoring cries of pain.

Lena ran.

Before she past three streets, this level opened out, and she darted down alleyways to hide. After two quick turns, she slowed, before the strange fleeing woman could draw the guards' gaze. Even after her breath grew less ragged, her heart still hammered. Perhaps it would be Erion who followed her on that journey—

If they were wise to her, now that Erion was crowned, she had every reason to act and none to wait. She had even carried the dagger with her—and perhaps they had learned from Erion what he and she had looked for in the library.

A hawk screamed, far overhead. She wondered whether it had struck down any of the doves in flight, and walked toward the library. Her heart calmed, but she felt colder than well water as she walked.

Guards, bristling with weapons, loomed on the library stairs—as
many of them as if they protected the king. They went in and out
freely, shocking Lena despite herself. Scholars puffed up like
bantam cocks in indignation, and deflated again when they faced
the captain, who had not drawn a sword, but who lowered over the
stairs as if he would strike dead with a glance anyone ventured in.

As if the stairs were its only entrance, she told herself.

Wishing she had slipped off her blue scarf in the alleyway, half-
glad that she had not thought of it and so did not face the strange
prospect of walking down the street without it, she joined the flow
of walkers streaming by. Her half-suppressed glances at the library
did not mark her out among the others as she slowly circled about
the building.

Every time she faced a new doorway, even one that was half-
buried in the earth, with a stairway leading down, guards stood
ready to seize intruder. As if they knew of the rope, and deemed it
wiser to keep her from it than to capture her.

Her stomach felt like a cold weight as she let herself go on, and
avoid the guards' gazes. Gawking was one thing—the crowds filled
the street to do it—but the guards would fall upon whomever
came close.

She had not sought out the rope for nothing, but it would not
help her now.

Her hand crept toward the dagger. Then she forced it away.
The guards were more guilty than a mindless snake, but even one
guard might prove more than she could overpower—certainly,
whatever the powers of the knife, he might cry for aid before she
killed him—and the captain had never been fool enough to set
only one.

She could think of a thousand things where she might need that
rope. And she could think of a thousand more things that she
might need for this. Trying with only the dagger and the sundrop
was only a little more foolish than if she had rope as well. The folly
lay in trying at all.

She walked off, more briskly, startling those about her and drawing angry demands that she watch where she went.

She would not have guessed that she would need as much time as she did to find the stair and the grotto.

Guards moved along the street and scowled at every passer-by. Though she did not know how she managed it, she flinched no more than an honest subject would, and they did not pick her out, even to give her a second look. Indeed, the rest of the crowd seemed to notice her no more than—she let her breath out as the thought struck—than before coronation.

Guards descended to the tunnels by ways she would never had chosen, until she wondered how so many could search when they had to guard two kings. Neither the guards nor the crowds hampered her as she wove her way through the labyrinth of buildings as gray as the clouds.

Finally, she reached the tiny square. A tabby cat darted off, across the cobblestones, and left her alone there.

Lena did not linger. She might not be alone for long. Her heartbeat hammered in her ears as she strode over, between two gargoyles, and down narrow stairs into air smelling of dusk and damp and stone. She had ventured here once, and for her own childish whim, when first she had read of it. She could venture farther for good cause. Her mouth twisted. As the king's only loyal subject, one could say it was her duty to venture farther.

"So. You did." The voice, echoing faintly from the stone, was hollow and despairing.

Lena froze as if turned to stone. Long moments later, she realized that she knew the voice, for all the strangeness of its tone. She turned. The gloom did not hide Rodvan's pale face.

It had, after all, been Rodvan who had shown her the tome that spoke of this tunnel. She swallowed. He could easily have worked out what maps she had consulted, to find a map of them all.

"I guessed." His voice was soft. "If you were truly bent on madness as the guards said you were, you would come here." He took a step forward. "My child, is not one of you enough? Erion did not imprudently throw his life away, at that."

Lena braced herself. She glanced by him. The doorway downward loomed to Rodvan's right.

Rodvan's words sped more swiftly. "I can conceal your odd behavior. Whatever any fool says, I can claim to know better, and explain more. But you must come with me, at once. To go down in the tunnels—the guards will never believe." He stepped forward, and spread an imploring hand. "If you are so lucky as to fall in their hands. Your path will take you into the underground, forsaken of the Glorious Sun. They are unblessed and the haunts of monsters."

"The Master of Heavens can guide my path," said Lena. "Wherever I go."

"My child—"

She drew the dagger.

He blinked and drew back.

"Now you may tell the guards that I forced you to let me." She closed her mouth before she babbled. Her heartbeat pulsed so loudly she thought she would not hear anything he said.

She did not dare turn her back on him; Rodvan might yet risk the dagger to save her. But sidling by him, swiftly, while his shocked face was still bent on the knife, brought her to the door. She hurtled down the way, not minding the shadows, trusting in her childhood memory, and listened. Her own footsteps echoed from the stones, but none others following.

As the floor leveled out, she stopped. Her breath sounded hoarse in her ears. Once it had calmed, her heartbeat drummed. The doorway showed in the gloom as a gleam of light, with no shadow falling from it. She turned her face away. Even the dim entrance would blind her, here, where neither sunlight nor moonlight nor starlight ever struck.

Other lights did, and moments later, her eyes adjusted, Lena recognized the gleam. Her breath caught. Sundrops. But even with swords and spears ready, the soldiers could not have prodded the scholars into a search; they would fuss and fuss and then search ineffectually.

Her heart started to hammer again.

Which meant that the guards knew the tunnels, with the briskness that they moved. Whatever they may have feared about venturing underground, to where the sunlight never reached.

She pulled her headdress forward, to muffle her face, and picked her way onward. The glints made finding her footing possible if difficult. Her own stone was near enough to hand to catch, if she needed to run.

The light reflected oddly, and footsteps resounded down stones. No one approached. Then, they could not tell she walked down there—

She started, and her eyes shut in a moment of frustration. And they would not tell that even by her light, since they had stolen the scholars'. For her to walk with it might even send them off on other ways, thinking that another soldier searched there, where footsteps without light would draw them to find the intruder.

She drew out her sundrop. Light gleamed redly through her fingers until she turned up her hand. It glowed. Even in these dingy, ancient tunnels of stone and brick, and grime, the light was as golden as ripened wheat.

The shadows it cast, from pillars, and through arched doorways, were darker than night. She picked out her way onward, hurrying as best she could. And always, off in the distance, lights glinted, and footsteps resounded.

She had yet to even reach a third of the way. One came so close she could almost make out the guard himself; she bit her lip and ducked into a niche as if searching it. A minute later, her heart pattering, she emerged. He had gone on. She might yet lose them, Lena told herself; she was not searching as they were, and could travel more swiftly. Occasionally, shouts resounded. For a moment, she fancied that her light footfall would betray her to the clomping soldiers.

Then a muffled sound, like the footfalls of a ghost, absorbed her attention entirely.

For a moment, her gaze darted about, seeking the noise in the shadows. Her hand trembled, and a thousand movements encircled her. She picked out nothing until the padding of footfalls returned. Then, light glinted from first an eye and then from a pale, pale face, surrounded by locks as white as lichen, and far too high above the floor. Vaguely, still in the shadow behind the face, were wings. Lena glanced down. A lion's body. Louder than a cat, at least. Her gaze darted back. She could just make out the scorpion's tail—or perhaps she imagined it, knowing that the manticore had to have one.

"Man flesh!" it roared, turning its face toward her. Its gray eyes did not look downward, or even focus on anything, but its nose wrinkled as it sniffed at the air.

Lena tore her gaze away and scrambled as fast as her feet could carry her toward the only passageway too narrow for a lion. Her heart hammered. She had come in search of a lion, she had found one—why had she been fool enough to try this venture? Hadn't the snake warned her that she pushed her knowledge too far? That escaping its poison should not send her in search of other monsters?

"Man flesh!" The manticore bounded forward—even a lion's soft feet struck with force enough to echo—and Lena scrambled up the stairway with the wind of its leap striking her in the back.

The walls shuddered with the force of its collision. One spat out bricks. The manticore roared, wordlessly, and the racket resounded in the passage. Lena, half-deafened, scrambled up and

THE LION AND THE LIBRARY

onward, and found herself facing a brick wall both more pale and more ruddy than those to either hand—as if newer—but mortared solidly in place. She bit her lip. And nowhere in her climb had there been a door, to either side.

She forced her breath in and out, and looked up. The light could not reach the ceiling wrapped in shadow. If she had only kept the rope, she might have escaped upwards. Perhaps. Her mouth twisted—if!

The manticore roared again.

She swallowed. Not truly a lion, she knew. All travelers' tales agreed on that, whatever other extravaganzas they proclaimed. A lion, thwarted of its prey, would seek out another rather than starve. It felt no outrage at escape—wasted no time lurking, vengefully seeking a chance to strike down the beast, or man, that escaped.

Lena looked slowly about. Then, carefully, she picked her way back to where the loose bricks lay. She put down the sundrop to free her hands. Once she had taken a brick up, she hesitated, but the manticore already gathered to lunge against the wall again. More bricks could fall, on her. She urged the light forward with her foot, to see that her shadow did not fall over her aim.

Then, her heart hammering, she hefted it up and hurled it over the manticore's shoulder. The brick soared out, brushing one bat wing.

The manticore did not turn, let alone pursue it.

Lena scrambled back. Her stomach roiled with the horror. It could trap her here until she died of thirst—and its blind face tracked her, somehow, as she moved.

Her hands clutched her skirt. After a minute, slowly, she took off her mantle. If it could see without seeing, she would give it a semblance more like hers.

She took up another brick to wrap in one corner, and make the mantle easier to throw. When the manticore crouched, ready for another pounce, she hurled it over the thing's head.

The tail whipped, faster than a falcon's strike, to pierce the mantle—and through, to its own hide.

It screamed in agony and convulsed. Lena snatched up the sundrop again and scrambled back as it thrashed, and thrashed, and thrashed. Bricks flew, and Lena cowered against the wall, clutching her light to herself. Fantastic shadows whirled, as if the wall were about to collapse and engulf her entirely.

Slowly, the sounds slackened, enough so she could hear her pounding heart—but a final blow might overcome the battered walls.

She forced her breath in and out. The walls might yield after the manticore died. Best to flee as soon as the manticore could not strike. At that, the guards had to have heard the ruckus. Though they would know it was not her, they might come to see what roused it.

She began to inch forward.

Boots echoed against stone. She seized her sundrop and plunged it away again. In the gloom, she looked away, into the corner, drawing her headdress about. She would not see a soldier coming, but her face was most likely to betray her. She did not think she was so pale they would take her for a ghost.

Indistinct shouts followed. She could hear only the surprise, and then the hammer of running feet.

A hiss of shock followed. "Her mantle—it's here."

"You saw her close enough to know her mantle?"

"You saw her close enough to know *her*? What other fool woman would be down here, to leave a mantle?" He pulled back, by the sound of his footsteps. "At least she's dead." He snorted. "And out of sunlight. Serves her right, fool Celestian."

"Should bring the mantle. Only thing that shows—"

The other one snorted again. "Should report back. And we won't if that poison kills us both."

"Captain won't like it—" said the other, but without much fervor. And the sound of footsteps receded.

Sweat beaded on Lena's face, and trickled down. Her heartbeat hammered out the minutes, and finally, she peeked over her shoulder in the silence. No light could be seen. With care, and little speed, she uncoiled herself, and her stiff limbs slowly yielded. Nothing stirred in response to the noise. She straightened and drew out the sundrop. It flooded over the brick, and nothing stirred while she blinked.

The walls might yet fall, she reminded herself.

At the opening, the manticore sprawled. It had smashed its stinger against the wall, and a pool of poison—bright green, smelling acrid—had trickled from it, and sent rivulets over the floor. Her mantle lay stained with poison. For a moment, her hands snatched at air, but she could not risk it, not when the poison might work at a touch. She would look a fool, distraught and out of her wits, on the street, if she ever managed to rise up from this labyrinth.

She forced herself to set her mouth. She would once again look a fool. She had already risked a manticore and the king's guard. Looking a fool would not kill her.

She still felt exposed as she crept down the corridors and their cool, dank air.

At least, no other lights glinted from the brickwork. The guards must have quickly found their fellows and told them how she had succumbed to the manticore. Shadows loomed, and she forced her breath in and out. What could be down here? The manticore would have eaten it. . . .

Except that the manticore had not looked starveling. It had found enough to eat among these brick walls. She doubted that many men or women were as foolish as she was, to wander down here, so it was not that.

And the longer she lingered, the more time the creatures would have to find her.

Her footsteps resounded with her brisker pace, and she eyed each looming stone. It would serve her right, if she lost track of her path, in all her pondering of soldiers and what the manticore ate than the way. She could only hope that she did not wander here until Erion's reign ended in his strangulation.

It loomed before her: a stone carved with a gnarled tree, one she had seen before, carefully sketched. She surged forward, the sight of it freeing her like the break in a dam to the water within, and snatched herself up a moment before she touched it. Care, care, care—the first carved stone she saw should not overturn her wits when any trap set here could destroy her and all her hopes, and leave Erion no fate but death. Holding up the light in a hand that trembled, Lena counted the limbs to either side. At the end, she knew she had not mistaken the way. She sent her hand out again, to lay it flat against the cool stone of the trunk. The carver had even made it rough as bark. . . .

Moments inched by. Lena contemplated how years might destroy more things than paper and cloth, how delicate spellwork could perish, when rock groaned beneath her fingers, like a tree in high winds. The stone shifted backward, to reveal itself a door. She waited, her heart pounding, and heard no noise within, once the door stopped. She looked in, at the stone passageway that ran parallel to it.

It held no dust on a flag-stoned floor.

This, Lena reminded herself, was not the treasury of some long-lost kingdom, buried beneath the weight of years. People came and went here; perhaps only Erion's kingship, and so the lack of decrees, kept her from meeting them here.

She straightened. That also meant that the traps could not be too dangerous for those who knew the way.

She stepped inside. The door slid shut, with a puff of wind that barely tweaked her skirt, and left her in air curiously scentless. She turned left and walked onward.

A man sat ahead, and her heart leapt and hammered before she realized that they had not set a guard here. The figure was too large. Too uniformly pale, even its clothing. Too unmoving—

though, as she crept closer, she doubted that would last. No man would leave a fine sculpture here for no reason. And she had read of some of the enchantments, though not detailed enough to mention this.

The light in her hand illuminated the statue, enough to show it carved of white marble. Something glittered blue on its forehead. Something enchanted. For beauty, they would never have used blue, even hidden in the treasury, and so it had to be for use.

The statue stood. As easily and deftly as a hale young man standing, without any show of stiffness, and it held the sword before itself. Its voice was deep and resonant, holding only the softest traces of inhuman stoniness.

"Who comes?"

All or naught, thought Lena.

"The king's betrothed wife. She comes to bring forth what is needed to preserve his life and his reign."

Her voice's echoes faded away. Madness, madness. King Halis had let superstitious fears, and yet more superstitious hopes, run away with him. Only a madwoman would trust her life to the web of lies he had woven to defend himself from imaginary dangers. That mockery of a coronation could make no king. . . .

The sapphire flared as white as the sun behind the thinnest of clouds—too brilliant to look upon. The statue stepped back and lowered its sword. For a moment, Lena dreamed of ordering it to let no one else in, but the danger of that order betraying her was too great. And she doubted that any of King Halis's servants would remember to speak of him as the king that was, or that the statue would permit their entrance even if they did. It was, after all, the king's treasury.

The statue saw nothing of her pondering. Its other hand reached to pull on a door that seemed heavier than the city gates, but whispered open beneath his grasp. From the first glimpses of the gloom within, jewels or gold or polished steel grabbed the light and sent it winking back at her. Nothing could be made out clearly, however much she peered. And not all of that gleamed white, she realized. Too much of it shone red for it all to be ruby, or glossy copper.

She realized, suddenly, that the statue had turned its stony face toward her, as if it ask whether she had lied, and had only come to gawk. It hardly mattered whether it opened the door, if she did not go within.

She strode forward. The pool of light about her lapped outward. Farther off things took up the glitter, and nearer things took on shape.

A gust of wind from behind her told her that the door closed as silently as it had opened. Lena drew her breath in and out—she should be glad of the security—and inched forward again. The nearest gleam was a tower of golden ingots, neatly stacked. More stood behind it, row and row. To either side, great chests stood, filled with heaps of gold coins, handy for payments.

The glow lay behind. From where she stood, the arched doorway was clear, and just a hint of the chamber beyond. She headed toward it. It was not as if she could bribe the guards for Erion's freedom with mere gold.

And if the king proved to keep salt here, why, she would merely remember that it denoted Erion's hospitality.

The ruddy glow increased with each step. From the echoes, a large room lay beyond—large enough to hold a king's ransom. She slowed as she approached, but not to stopping, until she reached the doorway.

All within was ablaze: suits of armor, both gilt and bejeweled; gold and silver ingots stacked into enormous towers; gowns and robes of satin set with gems; swords and spears and shields, all arrayed with richness. Gemstones heaped up like peaches or plums from a splendid harvest, and were resplendent in the fiery glow.

Slowly, she looked up, her neck arching. Hanging over all was a net woven, perhaps, from gold—it glittered—and caught in its mesh, the ruby she sought, enormous, perfect, glowing like a live coal.

Far, of course, from anything that a lone maiden could reach it from. Coins, and even ingots, the kings left where they could be fetched out, but the Lion's Heart, they wanted kept as the lamp in the treasury. She wondered for a moment whether she could throw the knife here. Then she wandered farther. She had known that, of course, that was why she had sought for the rope.

You could carry out enough gold to bribe half the city, an errant thought told her. Pile after pile of gold gleamed at her.

She reminded herself that nothing here, or even in the wildest legend, would ensure that they stayed bribed.

Lena walked father into the room. Her own light looked green in her hand when she glanced at it, but where its glow reached, gems and cloth showed moon pale, leaf green, the blues and purples of evening dusk. Even ingots looked like ripe wheat and not touched with fire, where their stacks towered, holding the gold that they did not expect to spend. She glanced up one heap. Over it, the fiery web gleamed.

Her gaze traced the fire back to its source, where the ruby glowed. She looked back at the ingots, stacked in a lattice. Then, slowly, she drifted back to the clothes. They were made of the very finest stuff, and laden with enchantment in every inch, to last this long.

Many minutes later, they lay heaped between two of the ingot towers. She sat on a chest, catching her breath, and hearing her heart pound. It would help little if she fell far, but it might muffle the ruby's drop. And it put the garments to more use than they had seen for many a year.

She glanced up at the ruby and carefully stowed the sundrop by the chest. She might need it again, but not to climb. After a minute, she went over to the plainest of the mantles, dyed a dark blue. They were not the rope, but the cloth was sturdy. Diamonds blazed along the hems, but nothing that a minute with the knife could not cut off. When the diamonds clattered to the floor, she set one newly plain mantle aside, to serve as her mantle in the street, and distract notice from her. The other fit neatly over her shoulders, and she eyed the ingots again.

What a fool. She rushed forward. Erion had days, but if she dispirited herself, he would need weeks and months for her to regain her courage.

The lattice gave her places to put her feet, but little grip for her hands. The metal was cold and slick wherever she touched it, and everywhere she could grasp it, shadows obscured her vision.

At least, she could slip her hands between them and hook the cross-wise ingots, though it squeeze her fingers to fit.

She took care not to glance downward.

Scrambling on top gave her one unsettling glance of far below. She crouched on all fours like a beast. Her eyes screwed shut, she fought, swallowing, to quell her stomach. She could not cower here when she needed to fetch down the ruby.

She opened her eyes and stared at the gold before her, ignoring the depths of the lattice. The ingots were spread far apart enough to make her footing dangerous. Moments later, she drew a deep breath and stood. The gold was steady under her feet.

The net gleamed with ruddy light, and she could gauge the distance between the tower and the stone. She would need to stretch but—she took out the knife—overhead, not to one side. Perhaps they had first built these towers to give them aid to suspend the net, using the gold just as they used the ruby to light the treasury while they kept it safe. They had to have gotten the net up here somehow.

After succeeding, she told herself, she might find an account in the library.

She straightened to her full height, reached up, and snagged the nearest cord. Harsh and metallic in her grip, it yielded not at all to her fingers. Only a faint tremor ran though the web. The light did not so much as tremble.

Lena brought up the knife. The cord did not yield to it, either. She set her mouth and began to saw. The cord shuddered, trembled, and began to fray. Lena hacked onward. Slowly the cord succumbed, until, with a jump, the knife sliced into air, jolting her.

She released the cord. The net did not sink. She turned to the next.

Minutes inched by as cord after cord gave way. For a time, she wondered whether she could have to crawl within the net, over the open air, to fetch it, and her stomach felt cold, but slowly, as the cords broke, the net sagged, and the ruby shifted toward her. The distance shrank with every cord, and finally, she crept to the edge of the tower to put her hands about the jewel. The facets felt strange in her hands, if its being neither coal-hot nor cold were unnatural. She urged the ruby over the last strands and took it as it tumbled into her hands; it was large enough to be awkward even using both of them.

The ruby glowed in her arms—through her hands, adding a new ruddiness from the blood. Even her sleeves were not thick enough to contain the light. She took a step backwards and sat, with it glowing in her lap and her mouth drier than a desert.

Long minutes later, her heart's frantic beat having slowed, she thought—down. The Heart of the Lion did little good in the arms of the king's betrothed. None at all, if she sat there rather than went onward. She took up the stray mantle and went to wrap the ruby in it. It fit easily. Shadows thickened about the room, though rays of light still lay rosy in the air. Her sundrop's white light could be seen—faintly. She eyed the descent and thought of bearing this burden on her back.

After a moment, she pulled out the knife again. The mantle was long, and cutting with the grain produced long stripes that could be bound tightly first about the cloth wrapping the ruby, and then to each other until she had a long rope of cloth. Then, slowly, slowly, she lowered the ruby over the edge and eked out each inch of cloth as it sank, the cord pulling at her finger.

And then—it felt hours later—she added inches to the cord and felt it go slack. Her shoulders slumped.

It took another minute before she tried to look about—not easily, in the new gloom. Still, she could feel the cold, hard gleam of ingots, and she knew how long the descent was. Wrapping the cord about the ingots, several times, and knotting with more knots than sailors binding the king's barge against a storm, meant that she could yank on it, quite hard, and feel no yield.

She sat back on her heels. Descending would have been harder, even had the light not changed.

And if she frightened herself out of it, she would die of thirst while Erion still lived.

Before she could think farther, she scrambled to the side, and wedged a foot in the first foothold. It would be no harder than descending rocky slopes with a waterstone, she told herself, and wished she had not. Summoning up memories of lurching descents that had left her heart hammering—and how Erion had been there to steady her, as he was not here—

The Master of Heavens guides my feet as he guides the stars in their courses, she told herself, and searched out the next foothold with her other toes.

The descent was dizzying. Her own shadow, cast upward by both lights, dancing and whirled on the ragged surface of the tower. Once, her foot slipped, and she clutched her cord, certain that it would fray and break. Only with difficulty did she force her foot back. The gold seemed slicker with every step. Finally, she glanced down, gauged the distance, eyed the footholds—and jumped. She landed with a jolt and fought for her breath for an insanely long time for a woman who had triumphed. And once her breath had been mastered, she realized how her heart hammered.

Still, once her heartbeat steadied again, she collected her sundrop. By its whiteness, she took up her other mantle and donned it, to look fitting on the street. The broach was stiff and would not fasten properly, no matter how she poked it, but, she decided, the mantle looked passable enough. Anyone who looked closely enough would already be alert to the strangeness of her. She gathered up the ruby, cradling it like a baby, and walked toward the door.

It bore no door knob—as if she could push it open herself—but a brass bell stood to one side. Lena rang it. A deep, pure note pervaded the room. She put both her arms about the ruby again, and waited. The echoes died off into silence. Then, slowly, the door began to open.

The statue, sword in hand, faced her. The gemstone had turned blue again.

She could boldly step forward as if it made no matter that it stood there, or she could boldly declare—

"The king has need of this that I carry, with all haste."

Her voice rang, without even a hint of tremor. The stone flared white again. The statue did not move.

"No, he does not," came its stony voice. "No good king has need of that. No good king desires that. It brings shame and ignominy on the kingdom. It keeps the the king from defending its prosperity and pride—"

It spoke. It did not move to stop her. Lena took a step forward.

The statue strode to stand in her way. The sword swept upward.

She turned and fled before the blade rose over her head. In the treasury's clutter, she might stand a chance, like a rabbit among briars when the wolf pursued. Moments later, as if the statue took that long to realize that she had fled backward, its footsteps thundered after, drowning the sound of hers. She darted about the first tower of ingots and plunged her light away in a pouch. With it muffled, the room's only light was the stray gleams that escaped her bundle and turned the room into a morass of shadows and lurid gleams.

And betrayed her to pursuit. Even the masses of reflections could not wholly hide the source. But if she dropped it now, all had been in vain.

She scurried onward, past the towers, to where the chests stood. There she hesitated. Fleeing about the room might let her escape to the door, still open, but the statue could pursue her down the hall. And through the tunnels. And even in the city streets. Until weariness felled her, no doubt. Or the guards did.

She whirled to face the statue and hugged the ruby closer. Dropping it might make it think she yielded, and it might let her go, then. To never return. To have no way to rescue Erion.

The statue charged toward her, its sword rising. She waited, and waited, and her heart hammered out the moments until the sword began to fall.

She threw herself aside, and the floor's stones hit like a blow. Only through the thud and the tearing sound did she know the sword had struck. When she scrambled up, the statue already wrestled with the blade, trying to draw it from the chest.

She had no reason to believe it would wrestle forever, and its bare hands could kill. She drew out her sundrop. Whiteness engulfed the room again, letting her see the door clearly, and the struggling statue as well.

She scrambled toward the door. The statue gave a great heave, and the chest shifted, and Lena realized that the man and the sword were one, carved from a single stone. The blade had not been added. The statue could no more abandon its sword to chase her than it could abandon its hand.

And the door already started to shut behind her. King Halis might never reach his treasury again.

And serve him right, though Lena.

After a giddy minute, she put down her burden to straighten her mantle and her headdress. Looking less like a madwoman would let her get to the lion itself.

Even if she were a madwoman. She looked at the violet cloth swathing her and wished she had told tales of a violet-clad ghost woman, and claimed to have learned them in the library. That would scare them off. She smiled, feeling reckless and fey.

Light seeped into the tunnel. Daylight, but revealing little more of how much time had passed. It could not have been days, or she would have collapsed of thirst and hunger and weariness, she told herself. She hurried. If she remembered the way aright, the square outside held a clock.

And, it turned out, not many people. None of them looked toward her doorway, and she emerged into a cloudy day. Hours had passed, but she still had hours until sunset. She fought down the urge to straighten her clothes and instead scurried along the street, holding the ruby tightly. Light would betray them, but a woman carrying a small package, even with great care, had obviously just returned from a merchant.

She had walked around seven corners and down scores of blocks, and up two flights of stairs, when a gasp made her start.

"Lena?" Anila scrambled up and seized her arm. "Lena, are you mad?" She gawked—at the clothes, Lena thought, not the bundle. Then she had a bundle of her own; their mother had sent her off with the laundry. Lena could even see her own garments in Anila's arms.

"What else should I be in a city of madness?" said Lena. Passersby started to glance at them; her heart hammering, she swept Anila off to an alleyway. They could not talk long, but having Anila on her heels would be worse. She tried to steady her breath.

"Soldiers are everywhere," said Anila. "And we don't own that mantle. And you're so near the palace."

"It hardly matters where I am," said Lena, but felt her heart hammering still harder. "If they are *everywhere*. Besides, this is also close to the—erstwhile king."

Anila's eyes widened.

"I'm even nearer to the evening house." Lena leaned forward. "And so are you. Laundry must be done, short of the heavens falling, but—why oh why do you come so close in these times? Here—"

Lena looked about and picked out one niche. There, she laid aside her bundle, took a headdress and a gray mantle from Anila's, and changed in the gloom.

"There. Bundle these up, all together, and no one will see it." Lena snatched up her own bundle. "Tell people that, yes, a strange woman clad in violet stopped you and questioned you about the evening house in a vengeful manner."

"In an old dress, like a ghost of years ago," said Anila, thoughtfully.

Lena smiled. An excellent grasp of it—

Anila spread her feet and braced herself. "Not without seeing what you've got in there."

Lena thought of pushing by her.

Anila drew herself up to her full height, tilted her head back to look down her nose, and said in what was no doubt the loftiest tone she could manage, "It might be wrong to aid you. My sister Lena would rebuke me for helping you without even trying to learn. That's the way you end up doing wrong, and in trouble—"

Strangling Anila would attract too much attention. Even back here, a ruckus would draw eyes.

So would a shriek.

"If you make a peep," said Lena, "you will pay for it with your life."

She must have managed an ominous tone: Anila took a step backwards, her eyes widening. Lena shifted the bundle to show just a hint of the light.

Color drained from Anila's face. She took another step back and stared at Lena's face. Her mouth worked, but not even a peep emerged. Lena wrapped up the ruby again.

"You—you—" Anila's voice was low—low enough to draw no guards—but filled with horror. "You robbed the king. That's magic. Only the king—"

"Don't be foolish," said Lena tranquilly. "I am the king's betrothed. I brought it out for Erion's benefit, as it is his for so long as he is king."

Anila's eyes widened farther than Lena had realized they could go. "They won't care if they catch you."

"All the more reason to divert them," said Lena. "Tell them about a strange woman in purple who concerned herself with the evening house."

Anila still stood without twitching.

Lena leaned forward and whispered, "And afterward, I will tell you how I did it."

It had helped, Lena supposed, as she walked down more streets, that Anila had looked like a girl who had seen a ghost. A woman in purple—half the people about her talked of that woman. Her mouth tightened as she came around a corner. They had not gossiped so when Erion had been chosen for king.

Then, Erion was a mere scholar, not a ghost.

Soldiers pressed by her, not noticing how she shrank back farther than prudence needed. At a booth, they seized the Solarian woman there, upsetting her stacks of headdresses over the flagstones and demanding to know these tales of this purple woman.

"I thought I saw her," Lena called. All the buyers and sellers stared at her. More slowly, the soldiers, their grips slackening on the woman, turned toward her, and their eyes narrowed. She pointed out a suitable street. "There. Heading toward the evening house."

Moments later, the woman scrambled to retrieve her wares before they were all trampled.

If only all of the guards converged that easily, Lena thought, as she walked onward, the other way. She would find it simple to make her way—at last, something simple. Perhaps it was only fitting that something be simple for once, finally.

Soldiers appeared, stalking along the street. One eyed Lena, and she started.

Before they could wonder why, she blurted out, "The woman in purple. I saw her—there." She pointed.

She watched their backs for a moment. It was even true. Her mouth twisted, and she hurried on. She had seen herself if not her face. Just as she had walked toward the evening house before she walked past it.

She directed another set of soldiers away from there before she reached a square where a statue of a lion stood, towering from the height of the stairs. Carved from ruddy golden stone, it posed with its mouth perpetually opening to roar. Crowds, bustling about their business, streamed about it, not a soul giving it a glance. How many, after all, had ever heard of its legend? She had not, not before Erion had read it to her. She struck out, over the flagstones, wary for any passerby. It would not be clear until she came close, but to go anyway but around would draw eyes.

A swarm of soldiers, far more than she had misdirected, came down a broad avenue, as if advancing on a fortress. Lena hurried toward the statue; she was close enough to look as if she took refuge, trying to get out of their way.

It did not turn their gazes from her.

"The woman in purple—" she began.

"That's her," snapped one soldier. "The madwoman who's given us that merry chase."

Lena ran. Three steps later, she knew she had betrayed all, but she could not stop. Soldiers hammered after her as if nothing could deceive them. One, pounding after, snagged her mantle. She tried to pull free, and the stiff pin came loose, flooding him with cloth. Thank the Master of Heaven and Earth that she had been unable to fasten it right. She sprang up the steps and clambered onto the statue. Her free hand reached out to snag a stony paw, and she climbed, the ruby a lump against her.

She picked out the carved hole, and a hand seized her foot. She kicked. The moment that bought her let her shove the ruby from its nest in the mantle, into the niche. It landed with a dull thud. Red light flowed from the niche, but otherwise it was as mute and motionless as any rock.

Hands seized her arms. Her head jerked about to see soldiers had gotten firm footing before they seized her. With ease, they swept her off the statue and hurled her to the hands of the soldiers below, whose grips were bruising. About, the crowd murmured.

"Madwoman indeed," said one, contemptuously.

"Perhaps our king should have a queen," said another, with a sneer.

Lena waited, quietly, in their hands. Even if she could have fought free, she had carried out what she intended. The soldiers did not even try to retrieve the ruby. And, as she stared up at the statue, she thought they had no need to do. For each marvel she and Erion had found at the library and then outside, they had read of a dozen more legends that had never existed, or vanished without a trace, or been so confused in the telling that they could not know the source if they stumbled over it.

"What did she put in there?" said one deep voice.

The soldiers turned, their faces set in incredulous lines, toward the grizzled lieutenant who spoke.

"We got the madwoman—what does it matter what the madness had her carry about?"

"Mad to *care*," said another soldier.

"Look," said the lieutenant, and pointed. "It *glows*. Any madwoman who can do that—"

Soldiers hauled her to her feet, and two seized her arms. The others looked at each other as if holding a sorceress and madwoman were a pleasant task beside retrieving whatever she had put within. Despite herself, her mouth twitched. A petty vengeance, frightening them with an enchantment that did not harm. Still, it pleased her that none of them even looked at the statue. . . .

Its fur rippled. Lena swallowed. Its shoulders twitched, and its paws shifted. Her heart seemed to stop for a minute before it hammered in her chest. She had not despaired at her failure because she had not really believed anything possible.

The lion did not cease for her doubts. Its shoulders twitched, its paws shifted, and she felt her breath come light and fast. To actually see the lion of legend was more frightening that she had dreamed possible.

Beside her, a soldier grunted and looked up. Then he froze, his fingers rigid on her arm. The other one gasped, and a moment later, her arm was free as he edged away. The knowledge rippled through the soldiers, out to the crowd. Shrieks resounded, and then the hammer of footsteps in flight. Even some soldiers fled.

Lena pulled free of the soldier still holding her. All could be lost yet. She snagged her mantle where it had fallen, for some dignity, and strode forward.

The statue's—the lion's—eyes opened. Slowly, its head bent so that it looked into the square, and Lena met its gaze. Behind her, the last and bravest of the soldiers fled, after the crowd. Lena swallowed. She had put a deep trust in the truthfulness of the books she had read, to stand here so steadily.

Then, no one would protect her from King Halis, if the lion did not.

Its deep voice rumbled, as if ready to shake the city's foundation stones. "Where is the king?"

"I will bring you to him," said Lena, pulling on the mantle.

Its shoulders bunched, and its words were growled. "Why is he not here?"

"His enemies prevent it. Set by the king—"

The lion frowned.

"—that was," said Lena, hastily. "The erstwhile king. The king who abdicated of his own free will and compelled another to assume the crown, and yet would hold the king's power as if he had not."

The frown eased.

"I am the king's betrothed wife. I will lead you to him."

The lion's head descended in a solemn nod. Then it rose again, and higher than it had before, to roar.

Lena's hands clapped over her ears. Buildings about trembled. The last souls, bold enough to gawk until this, fled.

The lion leap down, making the street shake, leaving Lena surprised that the flagstones did not crack. She forced her breath in and out, trying to steady herself.

"Which way?" it growled.

Mutely, Lena pointed. The lion surged forward, and she scrambled to keep up to her only protection. At the next crossing, it looked at her.

Instead of pointing, she drew a deep breath. "Once—we get close, we—may have to search—"

The lion nodded as gravely as a king out of legend, but Lena still led off, as swiftly as she had gone before, paying no heed to her breath.

Crowds had gathered. They murmured along the way, but the lion surging down the way, and the glances it gave, gave her a path clearer than she had ever had before through the city. Which was well, considering how swiftly she had to move.

The petitioners' hall, she thought. They even compelled petitioners—the poor, and Celestians—to present theirs to Erion. She wondered whether King Halis would void them all or consider them after. Or, rather, which he had meant to do.

But as that building loomed before them, in a yellowish beige stone with suns emblazoned on it to represent all-illuminating justice, a clump of men came down the steps: guards in their uniforms, and in the center, dressed more ornately than ever King Halis had been when receiving petitioners, Erion was manhandled along.

"There," called Lena, letting her voice ring. "See how his foes maltreat him."

The lion crouched, gathering itself, and bounded down the street. Lena gathered her skirts and ran after, unwilling to let it pass without her. If Erion did not realize—if he misspoke to the lion—

For all her short breath, she reached them while the lion loomed over all. Its eyes shifted to glance among them more swiftly than a songbird in flight. The soldiers seemed too frightened to flee, their mouths working silently. Lena thought some of them trembled. Erion, pale, looked at it. Then his gaze drifted to her, where she fought for her breath, and it was then that he started.

The lion's voice was deep and growling. "Who is the king?"

A minute later, the soldiers found strength enough to mutely point at Erion. The lion turned its face toward him, and its tail lashed. Moments inched by as it stood, its gaze intent on Erion, as still as if it had turned to stone again. Lena wondered—as her heart pounded—whether the legends had been wrong. Or, even if they were true, the kings had corrupted the enchantment, and the lion might devour Erion whole. And her, after.

The lion drew itself up to its full height to bow, its belly going down flat to the street. A moment after, Lena bowed as well, so deeply that she wonder that she kept her balance. But the lion must never think that Erion was anything less than king—her heart pattered faster than it had, running or facing down the armed sculpture.

Then the lion sat back on its haunches and roared again. It shook the air, and the soldiers staggered and fled. It roared on and on, as if not caring that it let the king's enemies flee justice.

Something moved on the wall's height. Lena glanced about. Lions—statues of lions—prowled about, gathering in a pride large enough to fill the square and overflow it.

The roar cut off abruptly enough that Lena felt deaf for a moment. Then all the lions bowed, and in such a mass that she could clearly hear their movements.

"You," rumbled the first lion, "are a just king, whom we may aid to rule in justice?"

"I shall strive to be," said Erion, gravely. "I am new to the throne, and my—councilors have done much to hinder me even thus far into my reign."

Lena let her breath out in a gasp of relief. Erion had guessed what she had done—knew what he had to do himself. She swallowed and tried to scold herself. Very few things indeed could have stirred up these lions of legend. Half the city had to have guessed what she had done, and those who had not—had yet to see the lions.

"Rubies," said the lion, with such distaste that Erion did not move, and Lena glanced anxiously over the rubies and topazes embroidered on his robe. "It was not the custom of just kings to wear gemstones that made them look blood splattered."

Lena felt a cold weight in her stomach. So that part of the legend was also true.

"A corrupt custom," said Erion smoothly. "Not, however, the worst of them, and so to be amended later, when time can be spared from injustices and injuries. Justice must be done. More, justice must be seen to be done, that all may know of it."

He looked over the pride of stony lions before him, and for a moment looked like a frightened boy-child.

"Three of you must come with me. The others must keep order in the city, as I can trust none of the soldiers who should obey me."

The lions bowed very low—to the king, Lena reminded herself, and bowed with them.

"Your Majesty, there was a guard on the treasury, but your enemies mastered it, so it does not guard as it ought to." She drew a deep breath. Erion seemed more shocked at her address than considering what to do next. "Let a lion guard it. I fear much gold will be needed, to spend and to cure what your enemies have done."

Erion blinked, but nodded. "Let one go, to guard the gold. As for you, my betrothed, my beautiful dove—" He smiled. "Come with me, as I go to face my enemy."

Her stomach felt cold and leaden. She bowed again, hiding her face. What had she thought would be done? Letting the king— Halis, she told herself—letting Halis go free could only leave them in danger. To dream that the lions' mere appearance would resolve all that they faced—did not befit a queen, Lena concluded. Even a merely betrothed one.

She walked meekly alongside Erion, a little behind as befit a subject, even one (her mouth twitched) of such high station. A trio of lions paced solemnly with them, either recognizing Erion's injuries or regarding haste as unbefitting to a king.

The crowds thickened so much that even with their escort, the people sometimes had trouble giving way. When shoves and scuffles broke out, the lions gave them baleful glances, and the crowds subsided into silence. Every now and again, roars resounded, some near, some far off. Lena could not be certain that all of them came from within the city. Her fingers tightened on her mantle.

"Much has changed, Your Majesty," the lion rumbled. "Passes to your kingdom have been opened, to the south and east." To the Solarian lands, thought Lena. The lion rumbled on. "Other have been closed, to the north and west." To Celestian lands.

Her heart pattered faster, and she glanced sideways at Erion. His face seemed lighter than moments before.

"I do not think their influence has been wholesome," said Erion, gravely. "Within a month, we shall open those that were closed. I must consider the open ones, whether they aid my subjects, but I do not doubt that I shall have several of them closed."

Sibilant whispers spread outward from them. Some of the nearest shifted a little forward, as if they wanted to appeal to the king, but then they pulled back. As the news spread through the crowd, some passersby paled, or started, or even turned to flee.

She whispered so to Erion.

He whispered back, "Evil has befallen the king. He must reign over a land where the greedy and powerful have done much to incite hatred and rage."

"And," murmured Lena, "the greedy can feign having suffered at their hands." Erion winced. She thought of how those who fled would be most marked by cowardice, but that matter they could leave to another day.

The crowds opened up before them. The evening house, in extravagant rosy-red stone, stood opposite them in the square. Its bronze front doors were set with suns in the sky. Erion strode toward it. Lena wondered whether they would have to hunt through its halls as if looking for a mouse, and whether the King—Halis—would flee, and if the lions could spread word of his appearance.

The doors opened, swiftly, silently. Against the room's looming darkness, Halis gleamed in cloth of gold. His jaw worked.

"That," said Erion, "is the king who was, who sets my authority at naught, though his sun has set, and mine is rising."

"You fool," said Halis. "You fool!" He raised his hands, showing a green gemstone as clear as any spring water. "Did you think that the true kings are such fools? To let the lions stand about the city so, when we would have no defense? That we did not know that taking out their heart did not mean it could not go back in?"

His gaze flickered back to the lions.

"You have imperiled the pride and glory of this realm, unleashing these monsters. But we are ready for you!"

The lions growled and crouched, ready to pounce.

"You will obey me!" Halis took a step forward. "Be still!"

A lion's tail, lashing across the cobblestones, froze as if the ruby had been removed, and taken all life with it. Gasps sounded from the crowd, and excited whispers.

Halis raised the stone higher. "Command the others to gather here!"

Nothing happened. Halis frowned, eyed the crowds, which started to murmur, and held the stone up the his fingers. "Command the others to gather here!"

The lions—remained still, Lena realized. Slowly, slowly, she put her hand toward the dagger. When her fingers slid around the hilt, she whipped it out and hurled it toward Halis. He started, and too late tried to snatch for the stone. It toppled from his hands to hit the cobblestones, and crack, the sound ringing from the stone about.

The lions roared and pounced. A moment later, Erion's arm slipped about her and pulled her close to him. She buried her face in his shoulder. She had not thought that far ahead—only to stopping him—and all that blood—but Erion could not have let him live, whatever happened.

Minutes later, the lion said, in a deep growl, "May all your enemies so perish, Your Majesty."

Lena pulled away. Erion looked very pale, but grave. The green gemstone showed only a little of its color, sitting in a pool of blood that trickled out farther, over the stones. And it was well that many had seen Halis come forth, and could swear to his death, because no man could lay a name to him now.

"I have many enemies, I fear," said Erion. "Many are within this castle."

A man came forward, gray-haired, gray-bearded, dressed in robes like a councilor. He bowed, deeply. "Your Majesty."

Erion scowled, as if trying to remember the man among the swarms of councilors who had urged the king onward. She could not, but she had never come close to the court.

"Much of the court locked themselves and above, in dread, as soon as the news came. They have few guards with them, but I fear that the stairs were built to withstand an assault. I know no way in."

Lena straightened. "I do. I must fetch it."

The rope of spider silk lay as lightly in her hands as it had before. Even Erion raised an eyebrow at it. The officials and guards who had emerged to hail Erion as king overtly stared at it. Some looked almost green, and glanced often at Erion.

"My gracious bride," said Erion—not glancing about, though he could not have chosen that strange address for her sake—"is it best that you use it, or should I have my soldiers do so?"

"Let your soldiers do so," said Lena. "Your Majesty."

Erion glance about and pointed out the tallest of them, with broad shoulders—one who looked uneasy, Lena noticed.

"Your Majesty." He edged forward but glanced between the two of them. "There is no grapple to it."

Lena held it out. "It is spider silk, and will hold in its own. They can neither cut it nor throw it back down."

But you, she thought, can climb it on your own. Enough trouble for me to get the ruby down. Someone else can do this.

The guard took the rope. A low buzz of talk sprang up, and Lena looked away.

"Lena!" Anila charged at her, and threw her arms about her waist.

"Anila!" rebuked Lena. "Is that any way to act before the king?"

There was an uncommon silence, and it seemed to Lena that every eye was on them. Anila sniffed, and stared about, not releasing her sister.

"In view of the danger you were in, my dear bride," said Erion, "sisterly devotion is reason enough for her neglecting it."

"But not for long," said Lena. Anila goggled, surprised enough to let Lena push her through bowing to Erion. And she added a whispered but stern injunction to keep silent before bundling her aside. Her heart pattered faster as the guard went to throw the rope. For an idle moment, she wondered if she and Anila should return home. They might be utterly useless here.

Then, she had not proved useless after Erion had been chosen as king.

The halls gleamed with gold and red and blue, flowers and birds and trees painted in intricate array. Anila's hand was clammy in hers, but not so cold as her stomach felt.

"In here, my dear bride."

Lena swallowed and walked into a room where the walls showed silver deer sporting among silver birches, but everyone clumped grimly about a niche in the back of the room.

"This," said Erion, pushing forward a dish where a flower had been ground into dust. "Have a care with it."

She scarcely had to hear that. A few petals had escaped crushing to reveal their form. She suppressed the urge to ask if he had foolishly touched it, and only said, "That is the black lotus."

"Black lotus?" said one guard. "There is no such thing as the black lotus."

Lena looked at him. "As there is no such thing as the lions."

A moan came out of the niche. Pulcherie, sprawled in disarray, looked out, but her eyes showed only black with the faintest rim of color.

"My love?" she said, plaintively. "My beloved king? He is well?"

"He—rests." Lena took a stride to reach the other woman, and found that her arm felt as cold as it looked. "Soon, you will join him."

Pulcherie smiled. "How well, how well—I could not bear it, you know, to wait in fear. So—it helped."

Behind her, Lena heard Erion giving order that she be attended until her death.

That would not take long. Lena let her breath out. Kudret had poisoned himself wittingly, and so had many others. She stared across the room, and it seemed very large, and she remembered that she was the king's betrothed wife. His queen would be expected to ensconce herself in such rooms.

With evening, the sun broke through enough to turn the western clouds into a flowery mead of scarlet, rose, and orange. On the steps of the evening house, Anila shifted her weight between her feet, like a small child wondering when things would be done. Lena could not blame her. She had never thought this far ahead. It seemed improper for the king's betrothed, that she just wound her way through the streets to her father's house. More, it seemed dangerous. But evening had arrived, and the air grew chilly.

"Lena!" Her mother hurried over the flagstones. "I heard—I heard tales—but—I didn't—" Her gaze went from Lena to Erion, to the lion. She only managed to tear her gaze away after a minute, to look mutely at the guards and officials paying court to Erion.

Anila grinned. Lena had never felt less like smiling in her life.

Bela puffed up, and eyed it all. "Shocking," she grumbled. "All the city will *ring* with scandal."

"Then there must be none," said Erion, his voice ringing. "It is well that you have come, Lady Mirjam, as evening comes. Best that my gracious and beloved betrothed and her dear sister return to their father's roofs."

Her mother bowed. "Your Majesty." Rising, she gave Bela a baleful, sideways glare. Slowly, Bela bowed as well.

"I will appoint a lion to watch over them during the night." One lion bowed to them. Erion, as if he had never dreamed of anything else, went on. "And to escort my betrothed lady to me again in the morning, for the Lady Lena's aid is needed. Many cases must be reviewed for injustice, and as she can read them and judge them justly, I will have need of her."

Bela started to mumble, too low for even Lena to hear.

Erion smiled. "The sooner that all is well, and the church properly consecrated to celebrate our wedding and her coronation, the sooner that happy day shall come."

For a fugitive moment, Lena thought of the library's being torn up, and cringed. Then she tried to shame herself: it was a church, and she had every reason to be grateful to the Master of Heavens. She glanced over at Erion. His gaze was steady on the great church of the Solarians. And—he had not spoken of *re*-consecrating it.

She tried not to be glad, but not very hard. Bowing, she said, "I go as you command, Your Majesty, and will return as you command, as well."

Even as the streets darkened, and the smells of evening meals spread from kitchens, Lena could see the crowds had changed. They had walked down seven squares and about three corners before she could put her thumb on why, but then, she thought herself a fool. More people sported scarves, or more, in blue, with stars and the moon on them. For a moment, she fancied that Celestians had found new boldness already, but then she saw faces she knew. She counted. One Solarian might be a fool, or two, but dozens confirmed her thoughts.

"Blasted knaves," said Bela. "Jumping to pass themselves off as Celestians."

"I am sure," said Lena, "that the king will not take such fraud lightly." She sighed. The king would have much to do, to ensure justice.

Anila stood in the doorway, looking at Lena. "If *you* are going to be queen, what's going to happen to me?"

Lena's mouth twisted. "I assure you, very few people have complained that they are sisters to queens."

"But I want to learn the library! If Erion's king, and you're queen, there's no one to teach me!" She leaned forward and whispered, "Aunt Bela told me I couldn't be a librarian."

Lena sighed. She and Erion would find it hard to even consult the library, no doubt. Perhaps they could devise some way to have her taught.

But the kingdom had to come first.

Along the streets, lions prowled. Great houses had their doors sealed with the king's insignia, proof that all within was forfeit, because the family had fled rather than face King Erion's justice.

People also moved about. Fewer, and more quietly, than Lena had ever seen before. And the blue scarves were yet more plentiful.

Lena, the lion, and Anila crossed the square. The lion walked with imperial calm, surveying all that appeared before it, majestically indifferent to those who gawked, and those who fled in terror, and those who made a low reverence to the king's betrothed and left her path with swiftness.

In a month or two, Lena thought, she would take those bows as only her due. And the easy path through the city.

At the church doorway, the great bronze doors were down. Artisans bent over them, with new panels, adding blue to the gold, and silvery stars and moons.

Lena walked on, feeling more unsettled. Her fingers came up to trace the stars on her scarf, and she pressed nearer the lion.

Guards escorted her within the castle, despite their uneasy glances at the lion, to an audience chamber where Erion sat enthroned, attended by half a dozen lions. His robes were blue and silver—and how the seamstresses of the city must have rummaged through their stores of cloth, and sewn all night, to dress him so!—and petitioners knelt before him. Scarves of blue and silver lay before the throne, mute witnesses against them.

Lena made her bow. Erion made no more than a hand gesture to acknowledge it, but his gaze met hers, and he smiled, so faintly that only she could have seen it.

"Grandmother insisted on it," said the oldest man there, his hair laced with white. "That we were Celestians who had hid ourselves when our eyes became dark."

Lena's eyebrows went up. A new excuse to evade the fines then. She glanced about and spotted the sapphire from the statue, retrieved from the treasury. It had not turned black, but it had darkened.

She pulled back into the Queen's Niche, ushering Anila with her. A chair had been set out for her, and a little table with paper, pen, and ink. Apparently advice to the king could be discreet. But she sat—Anila plopped on the floor—and reached for her sewing bag. Listening to audiences meant she could not read lawsuits at the same time, but a new scarf for the king lay in her powers. She and Anila were both at work before the petitioner stopped his plea.

"This tale can hardly please me," said Erion. "To have such subjects, who disown the Master of Heavens for cowardice and advantage? What hope has a mere king for their loyalty?"

Mumbled denies, and claims of devotion to their grandmother, followed. Lena appraised their clothes. If they had not done it for advantage, yet it had done them no harm. She took another stitch. If they even told the truth at all. They started to furiously disown any claims of having done it for greed.

"I shall take you at your word," said Erion, regally. "You shall pay a fine for having concealed your allegiance, and everyone shall know it was not for advantage."

For a moment, their faces contorted, but they glanced at the lions serenely flanking Erion. They bowed and murmured of their gratitude, and his gracious clemency.

Lena bent her head over the sapphire-colored cloth. She wondered how many would claim to have been dark-eyed Celestians, and whether any would be telling the truth. It was a moment later when Anila poked her, and Lena realized how wide-eyed her sister was.

Rodvan bowed before the throne. Her needle froze in midair. Rodvan's son bowed as deeply as his father—more so. Though she thought Rodvan looked the more frightened. When he knew Erion....

"You come shame-faced," said Erion.

"And why should I not? One among our number, admitted to the library, set the guards upon your fair and wise betrothed as she sought out the Lion's Heart. It could have been me, I knew she was about something, I appealed to her to cease—" His hands spread.

Lena's mouth was dry.

"Did you set them?" said Erion, coldly.

"No, Your Majesty. But what reason have you to believe me?"

Lena glanced over. Erion glanced down. The sapphire was snow-white, though it did not shine, and reveal the king's secrets.

"Peace, good Rodvan. A king shall not do injustice because it might prove justice, if only he knew what he does not." His mouth twitched. "You must have much feared my wrath, to petition so."

"No, Your Majesty, that is not the import of my petition." Rodvan straightened. "I told you that I appealed to the Lady Lena your betrothed to cease her madness and preserve her life. There is no way she could have succeeded, a mortal maid alone."

Erion cocked an eyebrow.

Rodvan blinked and looked like a stubborn owl caught in daylight and unwilling to retreat.

"Only the Master of Heavens could have guided her steps so, when she walked so far underground."

The needle slid from Lena's fingers.

"I wish to become a Celestian, and my son with me."

Lena slowly lifted her head to stare. He would not be alone, there would be many like him in the city and in the land, but for him, and him alone, she wondered at his purpose.

Erion sat as still as stone.

She bit her lip. As a queen, perhaps she should wonder what Erion might do, being king. To forbear, to let Rodvan pass without forfeit, because they knew him, because they trusted his intentions—would it be just? Even if it were, would it only cause discontent in the city, that one wriggled so easily to a place of advantage? Erion's new reign was not secure, and justice must be seen to be done.

A minute later, Lena seized the pen and began to write. A quick-learning page boy appeared by her hand before she was half done. Either he or her writing drew Erion's eye, and silence continued until the boy's footsteps pattered over the stones.

Erion read, swiftly, and looked up.

"It has taken you long to realize his providence," he said solemnly. "And whoever now realizes it, must pay a price, to show his sincerity. Of you, I shall demand a service."

Rodvan bowed, hiding his face.

"You shall instruct Lady Anila, my betrothed's sister, in the matters of the library. Without fee or gift."

After a moment, Anila clapped her hand to her mouth to keep from squeaking like a mouse. Nothing could stop her wriggling. Lena smiled and sewed on. The reign of King Erion—the Just, no doubt—would show more clemency than King Hallis's had.

The lions looked pleased. Her smile deepened. Then, with what they had done for Erion, the lions had pleased her; it was only just to make return.

Also by Mary Catelli

Curses And Wonders
Dragon Slayer
Eyes of the Sorceress
Fever and Snow
Mermaids' Song
Sword and Shadow
The Book of Bone
Witch-Prince Ways
Dragonfire and Time
Enchantments And Dragons
Jewel of the Tiger
Over the Sea, To Me
The Dragon's Cottage
The Maze, the Manor, and the Unicorn
The White Menagerie
A Diabolical Bargain
Madeleine and the Mists
Magic And Secrets
The Lion and the Library
The Princess Goes Into The Forest
The Wolf and the Ward
The Witch-Child and the Scarlet Fleet
Treachery And Spells
Winter's Curse
Crow Curse
Free Passage
Isabelle and the Siren
Journeys And Wizardry
Lifestone

Magic of the Lost God
Never Comment On A Likeness
One Name
The Drunken Mermaids
The Turtle in the Sea of Sand
Were I You
Where There Is Smoke